DINDLE

Dindle is a dwarf who grows up in a kingdom whose people are terrorized by Zoorndan, a ferocious white dragon. How Dindle slays the dragon, spurns as a reward the kingdom itself, and takes only the dragon's tail to create a world of his own is told in this entertaining story. You will come to know Dindle well and to admire his courage. His shrewdness and ingenuity in making come true his dream of bringing happiness to others as well as to himself will not only surprise you but beguile you, too.

DINDLE

by Paul Fenimore Cooper

Illustrated by Marion Erskine Cooper

G. P. Putnam's Sons   New York

Published simultaneously in the Dominion of Canada
by Longmans Canada Limited, Toronto
Library of Congress Catalog Card Number: 63-15575
Manufactured in the United States of America

10-up

For Cory and Judy and Sam

DINDLE

DINDLE

1

Once upon a time, in a little village in the most distant corner of a great kingdom, there was born to a poor rug-maker and his wife a dwarf, whom they named Dindle. As a baby he was ugly and shriveled up, and everyone who saw him knew that he would never grow to be of any size. His mother and father, who had waited many years for a child, were sorely disappointed at having a dwarf, and they wondered what they had done to deserve such bad fortune. But they could not help loving the child with all their hearts, and they set out to do everything they could to make him happy.

His mother treated him with such tenderness as few babies have ever enjoyed, and his father so adored him that he would hardly leave the child out of his sight. Even when at work he often had his son in a cradle close by, where he could watch his every move. Sometimes he half persuaded himself that Dindle was growing as fast as any child. At such moments he would measure him

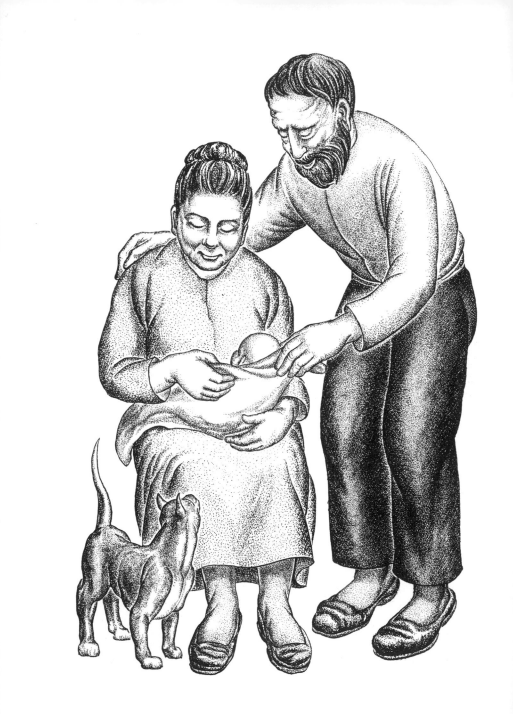

with a notched stick, but always he found that the child had hardly grown at all. Then a great sadness would come over the father. In some dark corner of his mind he thought himself to blame for his son's dwarfness, and he tried in every way he could to make amends for it. Dindle, of course, grew but very slowly, and every month his parents more and more dreaded what the future held for their son.

Now, to this kingdom in which Dindle was born there had come, years and years before, a great white dragon named Zoorndan. He had found a cave up near the top of a high mountain, and there he made his home. He was at once the most beautiful and most terrible dragon in the world, and every thought he had was as evil and as selfish as it could be. All day long he sat on a flat-topped rock in front of his cave, contriving harm and unhappiness for others. On the rock, in the sunlight, he was a sight to marvel at. Except for his claws, which were red, and his eyes, which were golden, he was white from end to end. As he breathed, smoke and fire came out of his nostrils and the scales on his body and the spikes on his tail glittered like jewels.

Zoorndan had not long been in the kingdom before the people knew just what kind of new master they had. Each year as tribute he exacted gold and silver from every village, and from the king he demanded jewels and precious stones. If the people did not bring him the best of everything — the best meat and the best bread and the best wine — Zoorndan lashed his tail and threatened to burn their houses or destroy their crops or kill their cattle. In his ugliest moods he threatened to turn the people to stone. He said that in his tail was a magic possessed by no other dragon in the world. By it he could turn living things to stone, or if he so wished he could give life to that which had never had life before. He never said what the magic was like or how it worked, and so often did he threaten to use it without doing so, that many people began to wonder whether the magic was really there or not. But no one dared put the dragon to the test.

So it came about that in the kingdom in which Dindle was born, Zoorndan — not the king — ruled; it was Zoorndan's orders that counted, no one else's. Each year he increased the tribute, and each year the people of the kingdom grew poorer and their lives became more unbearable. Only Zoorndan lived a life of ease; all he had to do was ask for a thing, and it was his. He grew richer and in every way more demanding; while the people, who had no choice but to cater to him, had to content themselves with dreams of how someday their unhappiness might be brought to an end.

During the first years of Dindle's life, his size did not set him apart from other children. He played with them in the streets, tagging along as best he could, slow and awkward and always last. Sometimes he could not keep up at all, and then he went home sad and upset. His mother and father, fearful at such times that he was sorrowing over being a dwarf, were especially tender to him. But Dindle never complained, never gave a sign that he thought himself different from anyone else, and the next day he would be out playing in the streets again. His parents told each other that such courage certainly deserved a reward, and they foolishly fancied that Dindle's reward might be someday to grow to full size. But, alas, he never did; he only became more and more unlike other children.

He began to look old and wizened. A great shyness came over him and he was reluctant to be seen in the village. By the time he was seven he had entirely given up playing in the streets and seldom went outside the house. His parents could see nothing but a dark and lonely future for their child. Hoping to keep him occupied and perhaps happy, they tried to interest him first in one thing, and then another. They met with little success. Like a weathercock, Dindle turned from this to that; from weaving rugs to gardening to carpentry to cooking. Each held his fancy briefly, and each quickly lost its charm. Soon the pain of having Dindle at home and idle all day was more than his parents could bear. They wondered if, even at the risk of being teased and made fun of, he would not be better off if sent out into the street. But neither of them quite had the heart to make him go.

Then, quite by surprise, something happened to Dindle that changed his whole life. It began one night when Dindle had gone to bed and his father was telling him a story about Zoorndan. Dindle, like every other child in the village, had often heard such stories, but never before one told with the vividness of this one. All at once the monster, with his golden eyes and red claws and white body, loomed up in the little dwarf's mind as clear as life itself. The picture was a frightening one, but Dindle would not let it go, and he made his father describe the dragon not once but three times. He would gladly have listened for a fourth time and a fifth had not his father insisted on getting ahead with the story.

13

When the story came to the unhappiness brought to the people by Zoorndan, Dindle's eyes filled with tears and he buried his face in his father's lap. When the father offered to stop, Dindle would not let him; sad as the story was, he would hear it to the end. Then, with a heavy sigh, he crawled under the bedclothes to go to sleep. The father, reproaching himself for upsetting the child, was sorry he had ever mentioned Zoorndan's name. But by then the deed was done.

The next morning Dindle was a different person. All he wanted was to hear more and more about Zoorndan. His mother and father laid his new passion to the story told him the night before, and thought it would soon go away. But in this they were mistaken. Each day Dindle's interest grew stronger and stronger. From morning till night he was at his parents with questions about Zoorndan. They came to dread the very mention of the monster's name and to wonder if Dindle would ever put his mind on anything else.

When his mother and father could tell him no more, Dindle went out into the village to question the old men. Almost any day he could be seen with one of them, seated on the ground in the shade of a tree or on a doorstep or in a shop, listening to stories about Zoorndan and asking questions without end. At these times he came out of his shyness, and as long as the talk was of Zoorndan he forgot altogether that he was a dwarf. The people marveled at the change in Dindle, but no one could guess what his questions were for. Occasionally one of the old men would suggest that Zoorndan had no special magic in his tail. Might it not be just an empty threat? Dindle would be quiet for a moment, then say,

"It's not an empty threat. The magic can turn people to stone or bring things to life. It's really there. I know."

Every day, all day long, Dindle was gone from home, off gathering new lore about Zoordan. In the evening, when he came back for supper, his parents tried to turn the talk from Zoorndan, begging Dindle not to take the dragon so seriously. "Why shouldn't I?" Dindle always replied. "It's Zoorndan that makes us all so unhappy." This, his parents had to admit, was the truth. They were far too kind to say what they really thought — that it was stupid for a little dwarf to fret himself sick about a dragon. For, after all, what could he possibly do to make matters any better?

Two years went by in this way. Dindle's parents held on to their patience as best they could, and the people in the village came to think of the dwarf as a little queer in mind as well as in body. Some of them thought that if his queerness spared him from being too unhappy about his size, it was all for the best. Dindle himself went his own way, content. All he wanted was to find out everything known about Zoorndan; until he did this, he had no thought of turning his attention to anything else.

Then, almost as suddenly as the passion for Zoorndan had taken hold of Dindle, it seemed to leave him; there was no more talk about the dragon. Dindle gave up the company of the old men in the streets; all day long he stayed at home alone. His mother and father breathed more easily. Perhaps, they thought, he will now begin to think about something useful.

Their relief was short-lived; a new passion soon seized Dindle's mind. By the hour he sat and drew pictures of

16

Zoorndan — now in this position, now in that, each picture perfect down to the last detail. Day after day this went on, until again the parents were in despair. They took a little comfort in seeing Dindle draw so well. If he is that clever with his hands, they thought, he can surely learn a useful trade, something like cobbling or tailoring. Their hopes rose, and Dindle's future looked a little brighter to them than before.

Then one day when Dindle was, I think, ten or eleven, he went to his father and said, "I know everything about Zoorndan. Now teach me to weave rugs."

The father, hardly able to believe his ears, said, "You tried that once before and you didn't like it. Why try again?"

"But it's different now," said Dindle. "This time I want to learn." And he begged until his father gave in and began to teach him.

Dindle learned in no time at all; it was as if he had magic in his finger tips. He made one little rug, then another, and then a third, each of the simplest design and each of such a size as a dwarf might like beside his bed. His mother and father, happy in their belief that Dindle had forgotten all about the dragon, urged him on with his weaving in every way they could.

Alas, they had been happy too soon. Dindle began on a little rug with a picture of Zoorndan in it. His parents' hearts sank. But by the time the little rug was done, it was so beautiful that they could hardly take their eyes off it. They had to admit that they had never seen such workmanship before. The dragon himself, with his red claws and his white body and his golden eyes, seemed to be woven into the rug. Dindle's parents asked him what

17

he planned to do with the rug. His answer was that he wanted to sell it.

The parents were not so certain of the wisdom of this. They were afraid that Zoorndan might not approve having his likeness in a rug. They suggested to Dindle that he weave a picture of some other creature. This Dindle refused to do. He insisted that little rugs with Zoorndan in them would sell better than any other kind, and that he wanted to make enough money to buy wool for a big rug of his own.

Despite his parents' misgivings, he stuck to what he had in mind. Whenever he finished a little dragon rug, he went out and sold it. This was not hard to do, because each rug was exquisite beyond belief. Almost every family in the village bought one; and to each family the picture of Zoorndan brought new hope, for in the beauty of the dragon in the rug much of the horribleness of the real dragon was lost. Outside the village not a word was said about the dragon rugs. No one cared to run the risk of passing the word on to Zoorndan.

By the time Dindle had made a rug for every house, he had the money he needed. Then he said to his father, "I have made my last little rug. Now I am going to make a big one for myself." He added that he had to have his own loom and a room of his own to work in, and he gave his father all the money he had earned. What could the father do but grant Dindle's request? He built a new room on the house and put a loom in it. There, day after day, Dindle worked at his weaving, as if nothing else in the whole world mattered.

Dindle's parents feared that now their son was going to make a big rug with a picture of Zoorndan in it.

Again they were mistaken. The rug was to have no dragon in it, not even the shadow of one. Instead, Dindle put in woods and streams and fields and a little village of houses just the right size for dwarfs. The streets of the village were filled with little people no bigger than Dindle himself. There was a mill and an inn and a market place. As Dindle worked and wove, and as the rug by inches slowly grew, its wonderfulness became more and more apparent. So careful and so perfect was Dindle's work that every detail of the village was there, down to birds sitting in the trees and to butterflies and bees hovering over the flowers in the gardens. It was as if Dindle had created a world of his own, a world in which he could live and be happy.

Nothing deterred Dindle from his task. From dawn to dusk every day, month after month, he worked at his loom. His parents marveled that he could still think up anything to put in the rug. The people of the village, hearing of Dindle's work, marveled too. Some suggested that he might weave on forever, always adding more and more to his rug, but never getting to the end. They pictured the little dwarf spending his whole life at his loom, ever growing older and finally dying at his task. Maybe, they added, it would be as good a way as any for his life to pass. Strangers who came to the village soon heard about the dwarf and his rug. Dindle's house and the room where he worked were pointed out to everyone. But no one except Dindle's mother and father ever saw the little dwarf or the marvelous rug he was working on.

Only at night did Dindle venture out of his house and into the village. Then he hid behind doors and hedges and trees, even in empty boxes and baskets — in any spot where he might listen, unseen. Thus he learned many things about the ways of men in the world, and all unknown to anyone but himself, he grew shrewd and wise beyond his years.

His mother and father could hardly believe the beauty of the rug. They had never in their most hopeful dreams imagined their son able to create anything so enchanting. They felt certain the rug would bring a good price. And it pleased them to think that poor Dindle could have, if nothing else, the satisfaction of earning a living by his own hands.

The years passed. The beautiful rug grew bigger and bigger as with heart and soul Dindle wove into it his dream of what the world should be.

2

In the years while Dindle was working on his rug, affairs in the kingdom went from bad to worse; there were droughts and famines and plagues, all blamed on Zoorndan, and many rightly so. The people suffered, and the king, old and burdened with his cares, saw no way to bring them help. Only Zoorndan was happy. Each year he increased the tribute, and each year he was more merciless in his punishments. The people, not knowing what might happen from one day to the next, lived in constant terror. The peasants watched the red sun set over their parched fields and thought of it as dipped in dragon's blood. But the king alone knew how close final disaster was.

Ever since the dragon first demanded tribute, the king had known that the day must come when his jewels would be exhausted. Now that day was close at hand. Bit by bit his treasure had been drained away by Zoorndan, until only enough for one more tribute was left.

Death, the king knew, was the penalty for failure to pay. It was not his own life that he dreaded losing; too little of that was left to matter much. What weighed on him was the fate of the kingdom. He had often thought that if he could free his people from Zoorndan, he would die happy. But to die and leave his people still under the dragon's power was more than he could bear. He called his counselors to him and said, "My jewels have run out. This year's tribute will be the last. Next year I shall have nothing to pay with."

The counselors were horrified. "Not to pay means death," they said. "At all costs the tribute must be kept up." They suggested that henceforth, each year, he buy in some other kingdom the jewels he needed. And they urged him to say nothing to Zoorndan, lest the dragon, knowing the king was out of jewels, press him to the limit.

The king would not give in. He said, "Every year I have paid the tribute, and things have gone from bad to worse. The time has come to take a stand against Zoorndan. Maybe something can be gained by courage." Then, opening his heart to his counselors, he continued, "Somewhere in this kingdom there must be someone who can slay Zoorndan. Perhaps that man, seeing what I do, will step forth." He spoke of his longing to die happy, with his kingdom free. He told the counselors that the good of his people meant more to him than anything else.

When the king suggested that a man might come forth to slay Zoorndan, his counselors thought him in his second childhood. They laughed kindly and told him not to be foolish. They insisted that no man alive, no matter how brave, could kill the dragon. How could anyone fight against a monster with a fiery breath? Any attempt to kill him would be certain to end in failure; it would only further bring down the dragon's wrath. The king replied that by slyness or by cunning the deed might be done, and then his counselors were seriously worried. They begged him not to be mistaken about Zoorndan. They said, " He is the slyest of the sly. No one can outwit him." And again they urged the king to continue with the tribute.

The king remained unmoved and insisted that the time had come to oppose Zoorndan. So steadfast was he in his purpose, that the counselors took alarm. They repeated that any opposition would only make matters worse. They pleaded with him not to be rash, pointing out that courage was one thing and foolhardiness quite another. All their talk might as well have been to the wind. The king, even at the risk of his own life, was determined to take a stand against the dragon.

On tribute day he gathered together his last jewels and sent them off to Zoorndan, with word that no more would be forthcoming. Inside twenty-four hours he had the dragon's answer: "Next year the tribute shall be paid as usual. Otherwise I, Zoorndan, will destroy not only you but the whole kingdom and everyone in it."

When the counselors heard these words, they were terrified and turned to the king. What good had come of his courage? All he had done was bring the threat of disaster to himself as well as to the entire kingdom. They advised him to reconsider and start at once to purchase the jewels for next year's tribute. To all their pleas, the king said no; not one more jewel would he pay to the dragon. When asked what his next step

23

would be, he answered that he needed one more night to think it over.

The next morning the counselors met with the king. They found him as convinced as ever that somewhere in the kingdom lived a man who could slay Zoorndan. His plan for finding the man was simple: to send out heralds to announce that the kingdom itself would be the reward for Zoorndan's death. And within an hour the heralds started forth across the realm to proclaim the king's offer.

The counselors thought the plan sheer nonsense and told the king as much. Not a man in the world, they said again, wants to be burned to ashes by Zoorndan. The king could wait until the end of time, but nobody would come to seek the reward. Secretly they hoped that after not too long a spell of waiting, the king would see the folly of his ways and be willing to make terms with the dragon.

Day after day the old king waited patiently for a dragon slayer, but no dragon slayer came. The king saddened, but still he clung to his faith that someone could rescue his people from Zoorndan. Each morning he felt certain that before the day ended the right man would show up; and each evening, when no such man had appeared, the king insisted that the next day would bring him. He comforted himself with the thought that his heralds had not yet reached the farthermost corner of the land. Until they had, there was still a chance for the success of his plan. But in this belief the king was alone; not another person in the palace agreed with him.

3

Then, one afternoon, there arrived at the palace a little dwarf. He had come on donkeyback across the whole kingdom. His clothes were shabby and worn from the long journey, and at his side he bore no arms of any kind.

As it happened, on the day that Dindle finished his big rug, the king's heralds arrived in the village. Upon hearing their proclamation, Dindle declared that he was going off to slay Zoorndan. His mother and father were aghast. In their fear for his life they said, "You can't possibly kill Zoorndan. Nobody can. Stay here and begin another rug. You are happy doing that." But Dindle would not listen nor would he tell them how he meant to kill the dragon. His father, unable to dissuade him, said in despair, "Then I shall go with you." But Dindle would have none of it. That very night he made ready for the journey, and the next morning, on his father's donkey, he was off. His last words were that no one was to touch his big rug while he was gone; no one was even to look at it.

When the king heard that a dwarf on his way to slay Zoorndan had arrived at the palace, he was discouraged. Had all his long wait been for nothing better than this? Often he had given thought to what he should do if a madman or an idiot came, but the arrival of a dwarf took him completely by surprise. The counselors at once grasped the ridiculousness of the situation and hoped it would bring the king to his senses. They gloated over the good luck that had played into their hands, and with amusement they waited to see what the king would do. They were certain he had no choice but to send the little fellow back home; he could not let him go on his way to certain death.

At first sight of Dindle the king was shocked. How could a little unarmed dwarf possibly imagine that he could slay a dragon? But a second glance told the king that there was more to Dindle than his dwarfness. As he stood before the throne waiting for the king to speak, there was trouble in his eyes and sadness, too, but his dignity showed the courage in his heart. At once the king took a liking to him and was filled with the warmest feelings toward the dwarf. He was quite willing to believe that Dindle had come to him with a plan worth listening to. He looked down kindly at the dwarf and said, "You are on your way to kill Zoorndan. Is that right?"

"That is right," said Dindle, put at ease by the king's friendliness. At the same time, he did not miss the mocking expressions on the faces of the counselors.

Next the king asked Dindle where he came from and

what he did. When Dindle answered that he came from a village in the kingdom and was a rugmaker, the king hardly knew what to think. He wondered if there were any connection between making rugs and killing dragons, and if so what it was. He asked, "What kind of rugs do you make?"

"Little ones and big ones," said Dindle. Had he been alone with the king, he might have told him everything about his rugs. But in front of the counselors he felt ill at ease. Suddenly he was seized by shyness. He wished he had never come to the palace; he wanted to get away as quickly as he could. He said to the king, "My rugs aren't worth talking about. I didn't mean to bother you with them. I came here only that you might see me. Now will it be all right if I go?"

"Why did you want me to see you?" asked the king.

"I wanted you to see that I was a dwarf," said Dindle. "Does your reward still hold?"

"It does indeed," said the king. And to make Dindle sure that his size would not be held against him, he added, "I am glad you came. Tell me how you plan to kill Zoorndan."

The counselors were delighted with the way the conversation was going. The deeper the king got involved with Dindle, the more entertained they were. The dwarf was harmless, of that they were certain, and he might be the very person to bring the king to his senses. They laughed silently at the turn events had taken, and waited eagerly for Dindle's plan. They never doubted that it would be either so fantastic or so foolish that the king would have to say no to it.

To Dindle, the king's question about his plan brought

27

new courage. All at once his shyness disappeared. He felt bold before the counselors. "How do I plan to kill Zoorndan?" he said, as if thinking the question over. Then he looked at the counselors. Already they were beginning to smile, but Dindle did not care. They could ridicule him as much as they pleased; all that mattered was that the king understood him. He turned to the king and said, "I shall kill him with my hands."

The counselors, unable to control themselves any longer, laughed out loud. A look of dismay crossed the king's face and was quickly gone. In Dindle's expression he had caught again a glimpse of the dwarf's courage. Perhaps, he thought, Dindle's answer was not so silly as it sounded. He asked, "How do you mean, with your hands?"

"Just that," said Dindle. "With my hands." He could not bring himself to divulge his whole plan. It was something all his own, something deeply secret. To tell it now would be to risk spoiling it. Yet he was sorry, after all the king's friendliness, that his answer had been so curt.

"With your bare hands?" asked the king.

"Yes," said Dindle.

Again the counselors laughed out loud. How could the king still bother with Dindle? Hadn't the dwarf's madness shown itself as clear as clear could be?

But the king was more interested than ever in Dindle — more certain that he had in mind a sensible plan. He said, "Just how with your hands? Tell me."

"I can't," said Dindle. "It's my secret."

"Then of course you mustn't tell it," said the king.

29

"I won't ask you again. I only want to be of help. Is there anything I can do?"

"You can answer one question," said Dindle, who had hardly expected such kindness. To the counselors, he did not doubt, the question would sound ridiculous. But perhaps the king would understand it. All at once Dindle felt as if he were a child again, back in his own village talking with the old men about the dragon. "I want to make sure of one thing," he continued. "Is there magic in Zoorndan's tail?"

The counselors could contain themselves no longer. They broke in and said, "No. There isn't." They begged the king, out of pity, to send Dindle away. They said, "His wits have left him. Let him go home and stay there, not be killed by Zoorndan." Right in front of the dwarf they made jokes about him and ridiculed him to the king.

Dindle stood there, hurt and confused. Again he wanted to flee from the palace, but even more he wanted to hear the king's reply. It was to the king that he had addressed his question, not to the counselors.

The king said, "No one knows the truth. There may be magic in Zoorndan's tail and there may not. I think there is."

"So do I," said Dindle.

The counselors kept their peace. Not only were they certain the dwarf was mad; they were fast beginning to think the king was too. They gave up all idea of further trying to curb him. If he wished to send a defenseless dwarf to fight the dragon, that was his business, not theirs. They had begged for the dwarf's life; their own consciences were clear.

The counselors' silence stirred doubts in the king. Courageous or not, Dindle was still a dwarf. Was it right to let him go near the dragon? He began to warn the dwarf about Zoorndan, pointing out how dangerous and cruel the monster was. In no time at all it became clear that everything he was telling Dindle, Dindle had heard before. If anything, it was the dwarf, rather than the king, who knew the most about Zoorndan. Even the counselors were amazed at Dindle's knowledge and had to admit among themselves that he was acting with his eyes wide open.

As for the king, any thought he had of stopping Dindle left him. He could not imagine how the little dwarf would slay Zoorndan, but somehow he felt he should be allowed to try. For a moment he wondered if his confidence in the dwarf had been bolstered by their common belief in the magic in Zoorndan's tail. Could Dindle's plan somehow depend on this magic? In his curiosity, the king was on the point of dismissing the counselors and talking with Dindle alone, but he thought better of it. He had said he would not pry into Dindle's secret. "You may go," he said. "After you have slain Zoorndan, come back here and my kingdom will be yours."

Now it came Dindle's turn to doubt. He said, "I may be able to kill him, and I may not. This time I am only going to see what he is like."

The king, afraid that Dindle was faltering, said, "If you go at all, you must kill Zoorndan. Otherwise you will never come back alive."

"Maybe so," said Dindle. "I can only tell that when I get there."

The king was amazed. Did the dwarf actually believe he could visit Zoorndan and safely come away, only to go back another day and kill him? Again he wanted to question Dindle, but he reminded himself of his promise and kept silent. Without another word about Zoorndan, he gave the dwarf his blessing and told him to be on his way.

Dindle said good-bye and turned to leave. As he did, the sight of his little back and his little legs flooded the king with sadness. He had intended to go with Dindle to the door and see him off, but now he did not have the heart to. For many hours after Dindle had gone, the king could think of nothing but the utter forlornness of being a dwarf.

The counselors did not share the king's feelings. They followed Dindle out of the palace to the top of the front steps, where they watched him mount his donkey and ride away to slay Zoorndan. For the rest of the day they laughed at the sight they had seen. Not one of them thought he would ever hear of the dwarf again.

4

The next morning, bright and early, Dindle approached Zoorndan's cave. The dragon, in no temper to be disturbed, was sitting on the rock out front, basking in the sun, his scales all a-glitter with sparkling light. Of late, only those who brought him food or tribute — the people he knew — were allowed to come and go. All strangers were challenged instantly and burned to death on the spot by his fiery breath. The dragon had heard the sound of hoofs and was on the alert, expecting a man on horseback. At the sight of a dwarf on a donkey, he could hardly believe his eyes. As was his custom, he blew out smoke and fire and ordered Dindle to halt. Then he asked, "Who are you? What do you want?" He did not wait for an answer, but at once began to sneer at Dindle's size. He said, "You must be the smallest dragon killer in the world. Where did the king turn you up?" He made such cruel fun of poor Dindle as you have never heard, and ended by saying, "No stranger goes away from here alive. Do you know that?"

"I do," said Dindle, never once taking his eyes off Zoorndan. He was so carried away by the dragon's beauty that he remained quite untouched by what had been said. It was exactly the same beauty that, years and years before, he had woven into his first little rugs.

"Then why did you come?" asked Zoorndan. "Is a dwarf's life so worthless that he doesn't mind losing it?" He breathed out less smoke and fire. In his contempt for Dindle's size, he felt no reason to be on guard.

Dindle stayed calm. It was the first few minutes of this encounter that he had dreaded most. He must get safely by them and soothe the dragon if he was to get ahead with his plan. He said, "I can't harm you; that much is certain. I am nothing but a helpless dwarf. For years I have heard of your great beauty. Now from the farthest corner of the kingdom I have come to gaze upon you with my own eyes."

"You came only to see my beauty. Is that it?" asked Zoorndan. He was still scowling, but his voice was not cross. He was little mistrustful of the dwarf's words, but he liked the flattery. No one had ever before spoken to him in this fashion. He wanted to believe Dindle's story; at the same time, he suspected the dwarf of having something more in mind. "All the way across the kingdom just to look at me?" he added.

"What else would bring me?" said Dindle. "And the more I look at you, the gladder I am I came."

Zoorndan curled his tail in pride; he had not been so pleased in a long time. He altogether stopped breathing out smoke and fire and said, "People don't often speak to me as you do. They usually curse me and threaten me and tell me how horrible I am. You see me as I see myself, the most wonderful and most beautiful dragon in the world."

"Indeed I do," said Dindle.

Not in a long time had Zoorndan welcomed any stranger. Now he said, "If you think me so beautiful, get off your donkey and talk with me for awhile."

"Whatever pleases you, pleases me," said Dindle. He got off his donkey and walked a step or two forward and sat down on a stone. He said, "You must know a great deal. You do nothing, yet you live better than anyone else in the kingdom. I wish I were as clever and as beautiful as you."

"I am the cleverest of them all," said Zoorndan. "Perhaps my cleverness is even greater than my beauty. I live with no effort at all. Everything is done for me."

"And you have such great strength too," said Dindle. "In fact you lack nothing. You are big and beautiful and clever, while I am small and ugly and stupid."

"That is true," said Zoorndan, uncurling his tail and curling it up again. "If more people felt about me as you do," he added, "all would be well."

"Of course it would," said Dindle. "But people are stupid, you know. Often they don't stop to think how lucky they are. No other kingdom in the world has a beautiful dragon like you."

"Quite true," said Zoorndan.

"You shouldn't be killed," said Dindle. "A beautiful creature like you should live forever."

"True; quite true," said Zoorndan.

For a whole hour Dindle sat there, saying only what he knew the dragon would like to hear, while Zoorndan agreed with everything that was said. Never in his life

35

had he passed so pleasant a morning. Then Dindle, as if more than ever struck by the dragon's beauty, said, "Your beauty is so great that it should be preserved for all time. Like all famous people, you should have your picture painted. Then the whole world could see how beautiful you are." Not for a second did he take his eyes off the monster, but gazed at him as one enthralled.

Zoorndan was more flattered than ever. He said, "I hadn't thought of it that way before. You are right." He puffed himself up with pride and curled his tail into an elegant curl. "Do you know anyone who paints pictures?" he asked Dindle. "Is there such a man in the kingdom?"

"I don't think so," said Dindle.

"There *must* be," said Zoorndan. Now that he had accepted the dwarf's suggestion, he wanted the picture painted at once.

"But I'm afraid there isn't," said Dindle.

"Then why did you mention it?" said Zoorndan. "If it can't be done, why speak of it at all?" At the mere thought of not being able to get what he wanted, Zoorndan's mood changed. He warned Dindle that his end was near, and menacingly he blew out smoke and fire.

Dindle did not move an inch. With the greatest calmness he said, "My business is making rugs. I'd be glad to go back home and weave into a rug the image of your own magnificent self. Then you'd have the picture you want and a rug to put under you when that stone gets cold."

For a while Zoorndan said nothing. Dindle's offer had caught his fancy and he was tempted to accept it. But how could he go back on his word and let the dwarf

get away alive? That would be showing weakness. He said, "I like your offer. But can't you stay here and make the rug?"

"No," said Dindle. "My loom and my wools are at home. I must go back there to work."

"But won't you need me to look at?" asked Zoorndan. "I can have your loom and your wools brought here."

"No thank you," said Dindle. "Your beauty is so great that I could never forget it. Every detail of it is stamped forever on my memory. I can work better at home than here. The rug will be far more beautiful if done there."

Again Zoorndan hesitated. He wanted the most beautiful rug he could get, but he could not let Dindle escape. He said, "Strangers don't go away from here alive. You know that."

"I do," said Dindle. "It was only the beauty of the rug I was thinking of. It must be absolutely perfect — just as perfect as yourself."

"It must," said Zoorndan.

"Then I have to weave it at home," said Dindle.

"How long will it take?" asked Zoorndan.

"About six months," said Dindle.

Once more Zoorndan hesitated. The rug had to be perfect, but he could not bring himself to let the dwarf go. He said, "You stay here and work. Then I can watch what you do."

"That would only bother me," said Dindle. "No one ever watches me weave." He insisted that he had to be at home to do his best work, and he tempted Zoorndan with little details of just how beautiful he would make the dragon in the rug. Then he suggested that he go home secretly; only his mother and father need know that Zoorndan had not killed him. "When the rug is done," he continued, "I'll bring it right back here. Then, if you wish, you may take my life."

"Take your life I certainly will," said Zoorndan. "But first I must have my rug." So anxious was he to have it as perfect as Dindle could make it, that at last he said, "I'll let you go home — but only to work on the rug. Let no one see you on the way, and only your mother and father are to know that you are there. Six months from this noon your time will be up. Well before that hour you must be here with the rug. The dragon in it is to be exactly like me down to the last detail, and just as beautiful too. Your life you must forfeit anyhow; but the better the rug, the easier will be your death. That is my bargain."

"It is a hard bargain," said Dindle.

"It's the kind I like to make," said Zoorndan.

"I accept it," said Dindle.

"Then it's sealed," said Zoorndan. "Now you may go."

Dindle thanked him and said, "You have given me six months of life. For that I am truly grateful. I shall be at my happiest working on your picture. I only hope I can make it as perfect as I promise. Then I shall have done something worth while with my last days."

"Indeed you shall have," said Zoorndan. He bade Dindle good-bye, and for a last time warned him against being seen by anyone.

Dindle mounted his donkey and rode away down the mountain, his mind filled with all that had happened since he left home. In his first encounter with Zoorndan, he had not come off too badly. To be sure, he had not asked Zoorndan about the magic in his tail; but now that he had seen the dragon in all his wonderful beauty, he felt certain the magic was there.

At the foot of the mountain he stopped at a stream to water his donkey, then turned off into some woods to hide until darkness came. From this place on, if he were not to be seen, he could travel only by night. For the rest of the day he curled up under a bush and slept. After the sun had set, he went on his way again.

When Dindle reached home, his mother and father were overjoyed; they had never expected to see him alive again. But when they heard about Zoorndan's bargain, their joy turned to despair. They could think of but one way of escape for their son: to get out of the kingdom as quickly as possible, away from the dragon's reach. They said, "You have gotten away from Zoorndan once. Don't go back. Let us smuggle you away to safety. Zoorndan need never be any the wiser."

Dindle could not agree. He insisted that a bargain was a bargain and that he had to stick to his word. He said, "Don't worry. My life has been spared once. It may well be spared again." He swore them to secrecy and urged his father to keep the donkey shut up in the barn, so that no one would know the animal was back. With heavy hearts, his parents agreed to all he asked. Like so many of Dindle's doings, this one seemed pure madness, but like the others it had to be accepted. Anxiously they asked him how he planned to kill the monster. They got the same answer he had given the king: "With my hands."

Dindle did not waste a minute. He went straight to his room and there he stayed day and night. No one in the village knew he was back, nor did anyone suspect it. At once he set to work on Zoorndan's rug. Again all the magic of his weaving came into play. He began with the tip of the dragon's tail and wove forward to the hind feet and the body and the front feet and the neck and the head. Bit by bit the image of the dragon grew, so lifelike that you wanted to touch it to see if it were real. When Dindle came to the eyes, he made them not quite true to their golden color; this he did in accordance with his plan. Every other part of the dragon was exactly like Zoorndan, right down to the tips of the red claws.

On the day that Dindle had set for finishing the rug, his task was done. That same evening he started off to keep his appointment with Zoorndan. When he said good-bye to his mother and father, he again warned them that no one was to touch his big rug. No one was even to look at it. The new dragon rug, Dindle and his father rolled up and tied on the donkey's back. For his own use, Dindle took next to nothing with him — just the clothes he had on, a little food his mother gave him for the journey, a needle, and stuffed in his trouser pocket, a handful of his best and most brilliant golden wool.

5

An hour or so before his six months ended, Dindle arrived at Zoorndan's cave. He found the dragon on his rock, waiting. He was not at all pleased with Dindle's lateness. He said, "You are none too early. I was about to send for you. At noon your time will be up."

"I know," said Dindle. "But I so enjoyed working on such a beautiful rug that I lingered over it until the very last minute. I hated to stop."

"Is the dragon in it exactly like me?" asked Zoorndan.

"Exactly," said Dindle.

"Let me see him," said Zoorndan.

"In a minute," said Dindle. Suddenly he was struck by the awesomeness of the scene about him — the dark entrance to the cave, the flat-topped rock on which the dragon was sitting, and the dragon himself with the sunlight sparkling on his white scales, as it does on frost crystals. If this were really to be his last hour of life, thought Dindle, what a magical spot to spend it in. Again he muttered, "In a minute." Then he added more loudly, "First I must find just the right place to put down the rug."

Where Dindle sat astride his donkey there was a stretch of level ground strewn with small stones and covered with moss and low-growing grass. It was in the middle of this stretch that Dindle planned to unroll the rug and spread it out. He was in no hurry. He could see how impatient Zoorndan was; let him be. He said, "The rug is woven of the finest and lightest wool imaginable. It must be handled with great care. I want to spread it out where the ground is smoothest."

"I want to look at it before I kill you," said Zoorndan. "Don't delay. You haven't much time."

"Very well," said Dindle. He got down from his donkey and put the rug, rolled up as it was, on the ground. Then he led his donkey off to the farthest edge of the flat space and tied him there. Walking slowly, he came back to the rug, unrolled it, and spread it out for the dragon to see.

While Zoorndan sat on the rock and gazed down in amazement at his own wonderful likeness, Dindle leaned over the rug, first on one side, then on the other, pointing out its best features and praising the dragon's beauty in every way he could think of. At last he said, "The rug is as perfect as I can make it. The dragon in it is so like you that it's hard to tell whether the real dragon is on the rock or in the rug."

"That is what the bargain called for," said Zoorndan.

"Yes," said Dindle. He was surprised and dismayed that no objection had been raised to the eyes of the dragon in the rug. Apparently Zoorndan had failed to notice that they were not quite so brilliant as his own.

Dindle's next move had depended on Zoorndan's taking exception to the color of the eyes. Now, for a moment, he was at a loss to know what to do. There was no hesitancy on Zoorndan's part. As far as he was concerned, the bargain had been fulfilled and the business was over with. The rug was done; it was time for the dwarf to die.

Zoorndan looked down at Dindle and said, "A bargain is a bargain. You have fulfilled your part to the letter. I will make your death a quick and easy one." Before Dindle knew what was happening, Zoorndan curled his tail up over his head and held it there, the tip pointing at the dwarf.

Dindle, speechless, was glued to the spot. He could do nothing but stare at the tip of the tail. He knew that Zoorndan was getting ready to turn him to stone. He had to stop it. But how? Suddenly his feeling of helplessness left him, and everything he had to do became clear. There *was* magic in the dragon's tail, and he, not Zoorndan, would take advantage of it. He collected himself and said, "Don't kill me just yet. My six months are not quite up. I want you to be certain about the rug. Come down off your rock and look at it closely. You may see something you don't like. If so, I have wool in my pocket and can fix it before I die."

Dindle's words made sense to Zoorndan; perhaps he had been a little hasty in accepting the rug. It might be wise, before it was too late, to have a closer look. He came down from the rock and went over to the rug, viewing it from this side and that, even sniffing at parts.

45

In terrible suspense, Dindle stood by. Could he now hope that his plan would work? Still the dragon, as if nearsighted, saw nothing wrong; he had only praise for the rug. He said, "It is a wonderful piece of work. I never before appreciated how really beautiful I am. Now, thanks to you, I can see the truth." And he sat down by the rug, the better to admire his own image.

Once or twice Dindle was tempted to draw Zoorndan's attention to the eyes, but fearful of betraying his purpose, he did not dare. His best chance of success, he knew, was to wait. Not until it had become absolutely certain that the dragon was not going to notice the eyes did Dindle venture to say, "What part of the dragon in the rug do you like best? Tell me."

"Every part," said Zoorndan, more pleased than ever with the rug and with his own good fortune in getting it out of the dwarf. "The tail is exactly like mine," he continued. "So is the back, so are the claws, so is the neck, so is the head . . ." As he recited the different parts of the body, he examined closely those same parts in the rug. When he came to the eyes, he stopped short. Dindle held his breath, confident now of what was coming next. Zoorndan stretched out his neck and stuck his nose practically into the rug right where the eyes were, more as if to smell them than to look at them. Then, in displeasure, he began to grumble and complain. He glowered at Dindle and said, "I take back everything. You have failed. The dragon in the rug is not exactly like me. His eyes are not as beautiful as mine." He told Dindle that by not fulfilling his part of the bargain he had forfeited the right to an easy death. He began to blow out smoke and fire, as if he meant in the next instant to burn up the dwarf.

"Spare me a little longer," said Dindle. "All I want is to please you. There is still time before noon to make the rug right." He went on to explain that the eyes had been the hardest part of all, and ended by saying, "I was afraid they weren't beautiful enough. They need more gold, Give me a chance to fix them."

"How long will it take?" asked Zoorndan crossly.

"Not long," said Dindle. "Let me get at it." He took out his needle and pulled from his pocket his brilliant golden wool. Then he stepped forward onto the rug and knelt down, as if to work.

Zoorndan sat by and watched. The more he saw of the rug, the more he wanted it and the more he wanted it to be perfect. He looked up at the sun; it was not yet overhead; there might well be enough time left. But what if there was not? What if the rug could not be fixed before he had to kill Dindle? The very idea was almost impossible for Zoorndan to bear. "Be quick," he said to the dwarf. "You have only a little time left."

Dindle was in no hurry. First he looked at Zoorndan's eyes, then at the eyes of the dragon in the rug. Then he slowly took — or pretended to take — a stitch. Again he compared the eyes, and again he went through the performance of taking a stitch.

The more slowly the dwarf worked, the more impatient the dragon grew. He was sure that at the rate Dindle was putting in stitches, the rug would never be done. "Hurry!" he said. "Can't you go faster?" In his mind's eye, he pictured slipping from his very grasp the

47

one thing in the world he wanted more than anything else.

Dindle, unruffled, looked up from his work and said, "To deal with such beauty takes time. I must put in just the right amount of gold, neither too little nor too much." Then he pretended to take another stitch and another, each slower and more deliberate than the one before.

Zoorndan could endure it no longer. Again he read the time by the sun and said, "You must work faster. The rug has to be done. I have to have it."

"I don't dare hurry," said Dindle. "Not with such delicate beauty as is in your eyes."

Zoorndan felt that he would burst if things did not move faster. To him, Dindle seemed to be purposely dawdling while the precious minutes flew by. Did the dwarf think he would be granted more time? In all his life Zoorndan had never changed the terms of a bargain, and he was not going to begin with Dindle. He said, "Can't you stitch a little faster? Must you be so slow?"

Dindle, as if in despair, dropped his needle and his wool and stood up and faced the dragon. He said, "I know my time is short. Only one thing will help me now."

"What?" asked Zoorndan. He was willing to do anything to get the rug fixed, anything but extend the time. That he would not do, even if the rug was not right when noon came.

Dindle said, "Your beautiful eyes are alive and stand out as they should. The ones in the rug are flat. It is hard for me to tell where they are wrong. That's why I have to work so slowly." And he stopped there, not quite daring to go on to what he had in mind.

"Eyes in a rug are always flat," said Zoorndan. "That's nothing new. What *is* the one thing that will help? Tell it to me."

"For a minute I want the eyes not to be flat," said Dindle. "I want to see them alive. Then I can find out where they are wrong and finish my job quickly." He watched closely to see if his words made Zoorndan think of using the magic in his tail — the magic that gave life to things that had never had life before.

If the words did, Zoorndan did not show it. He said, "No one can work on a live eye. That's nonsense." More impatient than ever, he added, "Exactly what are you trying to ask for? Tell me. Quick!"

"My life will soon be over," said Dindle, mustering all his courage. "Grant me one last request. Great beauty is deserving of a great deed. In your tail is such magic as no other dragon in the world possesses. Do this for me: with that magic bring the dragon in the rug to life just for a moment, that's all — only long enough for me to see what's the matter with his eyes. He can then go back into the rug, and in the time that's still left me I'll make his eyes exactly like yours. After that I'll be at your mercy."

"You ask for a great deal," said Zoorndan. "More than I have ever granted to anyone."

"It's not for myself that I ask it," said Dindle. "I shall get out of it nothing but death, whereas you will get a rug as beautiful as yourself." With these words he picked up his needle and his wool and stepped off the rug, as if to be out of Zoorndan's way.

Zoorndan hesitated. The time bothered him; there seemed to be altogether too little left for what Dindle wanted to do. But maybe if he and the dwarf hurried,

the rug could yet be made perfect. He said, "Is this the only way the rug can be fixed? Are you sure?"

"I am," said Dindle.

"Then I'll do it," said Zoorndan. "I'll bring the dragon in the rug to life, and send him back into the rug again as soon as you have looked at his eyes. But you can't take forever. At most, his spell of life will last for half the time still left you. Then he goes back into the rug and you finish your job."

"That will be all right," said Dindle, wondering if Zoorndan suspected his plan.

What happened next was almost impossible for Dindle to believe, though he was right there and saw it all. Without further words to Dindle, Zoorndan turned around and stretched his tail out behind him, right across the rug. Dindle stepped back a few steps and watched in wonder. Everything was happening according to plan. For a minute or two, Zoorndan remained stock-still, repeating out loud a charm, the words of which Dindle was quick to learn by heart. Seven times the dragon repeated the charm, then seven times he swished his tail back and forth across the rug. As he did so, a wall of mist rose around the edges of the flat space, shutting it off from all outside eyes. Only Zoorndan and Dindle and the rug were enclosed within it; the donkey was left outside.

In the next minute, out of the rug — and to life — came the dragon. By then Zoorndan had turned around and was facing his own likeness. An absolute stillness — like the stillness before a great storm — hung over the mountaintop. While the magic was working, the sky overhead had darkened, as when a great cloud passes across the sun.

At a glance, Dindle took everything in. The two dragons stood glaring at one another. Each was thinking how beautiful he was; each wanted no rival in the world. Zoorndan, without turning his head, said to Dindle, "Hurry up and look at his eyes. Waste no time. I want to send him back into the rug."

Dindle stepped forward between the two monsters. All he had to do was say two sentences, and the dragons, he knew, would be at each other's throats. He first looked at Zoorndan's eyes, then at the eyes of the dragon from the rug. He shook his head and stepped back a little to be out of the way.

"Have you seen all you want?" asked Zoorndan.

"Not yet," said Dindle. "I must look again."

"Be quick," said Zoorndan.

"I will," said Dindle. He stepped forward once more and looked again at the eyes of the dragon from the rug. Neither monster budged; both stood there as if carved from stone. Dindle took his time. He needed a moment to plan his escape from what was going to happen next. Then he turned to Zoorndan and spoke the two sentences. He said, "I was mistaken. This dragon's eyes are more beautiful than yours." He quickly jumped aside and hurried from the magic spot, through the mist, and into Zoorndan's cave. He knew what he had started, but he dared not wait to see it finished.

Hardly was Dindle out of sight when the dragon from the rug curled his tail into a magnificent curl and puffed himself up and said, "I knew it. I am the most beautiful dragon in the world."

"You're not," said Zoorndan. "I am."

"My eyes are more beautiful than yours," said the dragon from the rug.

"They're not," said Zoorndan. "No eyes are more beautiful than mine." In his rage, he forgot about the dwarf; he forgot about the rug; he forgot about everything but his hatred of the dragon who faced him.

In the next minute, as Dindle had planned, the two monsters fell to fighting. No one saw them, so no one knows exactly what the fight was like. To Dindle, safe in the cave, came the horrible sounds of the dragons' battle. Much as he wanted to see who was winning, he dared not leave his hiding place. For exactly twelve minutes the fight went on. Then there was utter silence. The smoke of battle lifted; the wall of mist disappeared. When Dindle came out from the cave, the dragon from the rug was back in the rug and Zoorndan's lifeless body lay stretched out on the ground.

For a moment Dindle felt a kind of sorrow for Zoorndan. Perhaps, he thought to himself, to be too big is in some ways as bad as to be too small. By now the darkened sky had cleared and the sun was shining with a new and fresh brightness. Its rays fell on Zoorndan's lifeless body, but no longer did the white scales glisten; no longer did the golden eyes shine.

Dindle turned away from the dragon and went once more into the cave. There he found all the jewels and gold and silver — all the tribute Zoorndan had exacted from the king and his people. These, Dindle said to himself, must go back to those they came from; the jewels

to the king, the gold and silver to the people. His heart quickened at the thought, and through his mind ran the thousand and one glad tidings that would spread across the realm now that Zoorndan was dead.

He went out of the cave and mounted his donkey and started down the trail. He left everything in the clearing just as it was. He had to see the king and settle with him about the reward. Then there were two or three little requests he wished to make. These, he was certain, no one would now have the heart to refuse him, not even the counselors.

6

The king, although Dindle did not appear again, never quite gave him up as dead. He believed that the dwarf might have gone to see Zoorndan and come away, and was still waiting somewhere to go back and kill him. But if he was waiting, no one could say where, for no one except his mother and father had seen hide nor hair of the dwarf since he last left the palace. The more the counselors pressed the king to forget Dindle and begin buying jewels for the next tribute, the less he was inclined to do so. Month after month, on the chance that Dindle was still alive, he put the counselors off, until their patience was at an end. They were threatening to arrange for the tribute themselves when word was brought in that Dindle was at the palace. The king took new heart.

But not the counselors. They were sure the dwarf had been nowhere near Zoorndan. They wondered what story he would tell this time. As he came into the room they eyed him with contempt. They hoped that the king would at last see that Dindle was nothing but an unfortunate little dwarf, and that there would be an end to all the foolish talk about his courage.

Dindle walked forward, bowed low, and stood in silence. On the way down the mountain he had rehearsed how he would break the news to the king. But at this moment, as he stood there, he forgot the words. Suddenly the whole last six months seemed like a dream. Had he really killed the dragon? Was Zoorndan really lying dead in front of his cave? Just then he heard the king's voice, and quicker than it takes to tell, he collected his wits, and the words he had rehearsed came back to him.

"I had almost given you up for dead," the king was saying. "What happened?"

"Everything went just as I had planned it," said Dindle.

"How was that?" asked the king, certain the dwarf could not mean that he had slain Zoorndan.

"The first time," said Dindle, "I went just to see Zoorndan, not to kill him." A quick look at the counselors told him that no matter what he said, they were ready to disbelieve it.

"You went to see Zoorndan," said the king. "And came away with your life."

"I did," said Dindle.

"How?" asked the king.

"It was easy," said Dindle. He explained about his rugmaking and how he had spent most of his life working on a big rug for himself. Then he told of his visit to Zoorndan and all about the picture the dragon wanted, and he described the monster in such detail as to leave no doubt that he spoke the truth. He ended with an account of the bargain he had struck and of his time at home working on the dragon rug.

The king said nothing. Already he was certain that Dindle's story would end with the slaying of the dragon, and he leaned forward so as not to miss a word. The counselors moved uneasily in their seats. They, too, had heard the ring of truth in Dindle's words and each was wondering what his place would be in a kingdom ruled over by a dwarf.

Dindle quickly moved on to the story's second part. Encouraged by the king's intentness, he continued with words that fairly tumbled from his mouth. He said. "I went the first time to see Zoorndan; the second time I went to kill him." In a silence as deep as the silence that fell when Zoorndan used the magic in his tail, Dindle went on and told what had happened. Not a detail did he skip; not a single incident did he leave out. He told it all so plainly that the king and the counselors could as well have been at the scene itself. At the end he was silent for a moment, then he held out his hands and said, "With these hands I have slain Zoorndan."

The king did not hesitate. Without even a look at his counselors, he rose from his throne and said to Dindle, "Be seated here. My kingdom is yours."

The counselors, appalled at the speed with which events were moving, looked unbelieving at the king. How dared he act in such haste and without their advice? They were about to ask him to sit down and reconsider his offer, when Dindle took the words out of their mouths. "Please sit down again," he said to the king. "The throne of this kingdom is not for me."

"Why not?" asked the king. "You have slain Zoorn-dan; the reward is yours." And he urged Dindle not to draw back from accepting what was rightly his.

While the king spoke thus, Dindle stood shaking his head in refusal. "I can't accept it," he said. "I really can't."

"Why not?" the king asked again.

"I already have a kingdom of my own," said Dindle.

The king was completely baffled. "What kingdom?" he asked. "Where?"

"It's in a rug," said Dindle, hesitantly. No sooner had he said it than he realized how foolish it must have sounded, and his face reddened. The counselors laughed, and Dindle could see that the king was beginning to think him mad. In his confusion he abruptly changed the subject and said, "I don't want your kingdom as a reward. All I want is the dragon's tail."

The king gasped. First a kingdom in a rug, then a dragon's tail for a reward! What on earth could be the matter with Dindle to have earned a kingdom and to ask for only Zoorndan's tail? But the king pursued the point no further. He promised to get the dragon's tail; also, at the dwarf's request, to have the dragon rug brought to the palace and to dispatch men to Dindle's village for the big rug that was there.

The counselors were ordered to send heralds forth to proclaim that Dindle had slain Zoorndan. The king caused to be returned to each village its share of the gold and silver tribute. As the heralds went across the land, great was the rejoicing everywhere, and on every-body's lips was Dindle's name.

To the men who went to his home, Dindle entrusted a message for his mother and father. It said:

> With my own hands I have killed Zoorndan. Please give the bearers of this message my big rug to bring back here to the palace. For a month I shall stay with the king; then I shall go away, but to where, no one must know. In time you will receive from me a token. Then will you be able to come and see me in my happiness.

Dindle closed the message with his love, and wished them good fortune.

The king, as he had promised, had the dragon rug and the dragon's tail brought to the palace. The tail was left on the front lawn for the curious to see, full proof that Zoorndan was dead. Dindle was so courted and so entertained that many a day he longed to escape and be off by himself. Kind as the people in the palace were, he felt his difference from them. And though not a single person, by look or by word, hinted at his size, he was more conscious than ever before that he was a dwarf.

In time the big rug arrived, and at the end of a month Dindle said to the king, "Tomorrow I must leave you." He asked for seven men to go with him on his journey, and a wagon to carry the dragon's tail and the big rug. The beautiful dragon rug he gave to the king; at the same time he told him — and for his ears only — what he planned to do with his own big rug. That night Dindle went to bed happy.

The next morning Dindle and his party were off. Six of the king's best horses were hitched to the wagon, laden with the big rug and the dragon's tail. On the seat beside the driver sat Dindle himself; only he knew where they were going. The king, who knew he would never see the dwarf again, was sad; the others who had come to say good-bye were amused at so strange a load being taken on a journey.

For many, many days Dindle journeyed across the kingdom, following first one road then another until in time he came to a country of beautiful hills. Among these hills no road ran, but so open was the country that Dindle and the king's men could still drive on. At last, deep in among the hills, they came to such a lovely valley as was to be found nowhere else in the land. Here Dindle bade the driver stop, and he ordered the men to unload the rug and the dragon's tail. He said, "It is here that I shall stay forever." On a flat spot he had carefully chosen, he had the men unroll the big rug and spread it out.

Then for the first time did anyone see the whole rug. When it was spread out, the king's men were spellbound. As they stared at the rug, the village in it and the woods and the fields seemed real and they knew the rug to be a world that Dindle had woven for himself. In one and the same instant, all seven men understood what it was that Dindle now hoped he could do. They could hardly wait to see how he would go about it.

Dindle directed them to pull the rug this way and that until its position satisfied him. Then he said, "Take the horses and the wagon away. Tie them up over there." And he pointed to a spot some distance off. When the men came back, Dindle said, "Now you must do exactly as I tell you. No one but me must say a word." He had the men pick up the dragon's tail, and holding on to the big end, cast out the tail so that it lay full length across the rug. When this had been done, Dindle stood by and — seven times — slowly repeated the charm he had heard Zoorndan say. Then he told the men to swish the tail back and forth across the rug seven times. But nothing happened.

Dindle's eyes filled with tears. Could it be that, dead, there was no magic in the tail? After all he had done, did he now have to abandon his dream? Maybe, he thought, I have done something wrong. Perhaps the magic will work only if I am alone with the rug. Or perhaps it will work only when everything else has been taken care of. He remembered the token he had promised his parents. If he gave the token to the king's men and sent them away out of the valley, then his big rug might come to life.

With these thoughts he took out his knife and cut off the very tip of the dragon's tail and handed it to the driver. "This is for my parents," he said. "Please ask the king to send it to them." He told the men that he wished to be by himself, and ordered them to leave with their wagon as quickly as possible. He warned them that once they were out of the valley, they would be unable to remember where they had been. With that he thanked them and sent them on their way.

The men had not been gone long when a silvery mist began to fill the valley from all sides. Dindle, seeing it, knew that Zoorndan's tail had not lost its magic. He stepped to the middle of the rug and waited.

The mist closed in on Dindle and his rug. Then all about him, the world that Dindle had woven came into

being. The houses of the village in his rug rose on both sides of the streets, the trees stood up, the grass grew in the fields, and the streams began to run. To Dindle's ears came the sounds of awakening life: birds sang in the trees, dogs barked, and people stirred and talked in the streets. Listening, Dindle heard somewhere in the distance the sound of a water wheel turning and dripping, and he knew that the millstones had begun to grind. Peering through the silvery mist, he saw the creation of his own new world. It was like watching at the dawn of time, when all new things were made. How long he stood there even Dindle was never certain — perhaps a few minutes, perhaps a lot longer. Then the mist cleared away and Dindle was standing in the street in his own village, among people of his own size and kind, in a world of his own making. Today he is king and rules with a gentleness and a kindness not known to any other kingdom on earth.

The king's men, exactly as Dindle had said, forgot where they had been. When they reached the palace, they gave the tip of Zoorndan's tail to the king, and he in turn sent it to Dindle's mother and father. It was a very special gift. When Dindle's father puts it in his pocket, the tip of the dragon's tail makes it possible for him and Dindle's mother to find their way to their son's village. They go there and themselves grow small, and each year spend many happy weeks with Dindle. No one is the wiser as to where they go, for like the good parents they are, they guard their son's secret with their very lives.

The Author

PAUL FENIMORE COOPER, a great-grandson of the famous American novelist, lives in Cooperstown, New York. Educated at Taft School, Yale, and Trinity College, Cambridge, he has long been fascinated by the Arctic. After a number of flights to the Polar Sea, he decided to write a book about King William Island and to put into it the story of the North that has always fascinated him. The result was *Island of the Lost*. Mr. Cooper has also written a story for young people, *Tal*.